S0-AJR-074

Explorers & Exploration

The Travels of
Sieur de La Salle

By Lara Bergen
Illustrated by Patrick O'Brien

Raintree Steck-Vaughn Publishers

A Harcourt Company

Austin · New York
www.steck-vaughn.com

Published by Raintree Steck-Vaughn Publishers,
an imprint of Steck-Vaughn Company

Library of Congress Cataloging-in-Publication Data
Bergen, Lara Rice
    Sieur de La Salle/by Lara Bergen.
        p. cm. — (Explorers and exploration)
    Includes index.
    ISBN 0-7398-1495-8
        1. La Salle, Robert Cavelier, sieur de, 1643–1687—Juvenile literature.
2. Explorers—North America—Biography—Juvenile literature.
3. Explorers—France—Biography—Juvenile literature.   4. Canada—
History—To 1763 (New France)—Juvenile literature.   5. Mississippi
River Valley—Discovery and exploration—French—Juvenile literature.
[1. La Salle, Robert Cavelier, sieur de, 1643-1687. 2. Explorers.
3. Mississippi River—Discovery and exploration.]
I. Title. II. Series.

F1030.5 .B47 2000
970.01'8'092—dc21   00-041943

Printed and bound in the United States of America
10 9 8 7 6 5 4 3 2 1 W 04 03 02 01

Produced by By George Productions, Inc.

Illustration Acknowledgments:
pp 5, 18, 25, 31, 37, and 42, North Wind Picture Archives; pp 9, 20, 32, 35, 39, and 41, The New York Public Library.
All other artwork is by Patrick O'Brien.

Contents

Looking for a Life of Adventure

The French explorer who today is known as Sieur de La Salle was born René-Robert Cavelier. He received the title "sieur," or "sir," as an adult. The name "La Salle" was taken from the name of his family's estate.

By the time La Salle was born in Rouen, France, in 1643, England, Spain, and France had each claimed part of North America. Spain had claimed the southern part of North America, from what is now Florida to the Pacific Ocean. The English had claimed the east coast. And the French had claimed the area in the north where Canada is today. They called it New France. The west, however, was still a mystery to Europeans. Growing up, La Salle heard many stories about the Americas.

René-Robert Cavelier was born in Rouen, France.

La Salle was wealthy, and he was sent to the best schools, run by Jesuit priests. Jesuits were one of the most educated groups of Catholic missionaries. They were also one of the most adventurous. They gave La Salle a wish to travel and explore.

After graduating from college, La Salle became a teacher at a Jesuit school. However, teaching bored him. He did not like being shut up in a room full of students. He wanted to see the world!

When he was only 22, La Salle begged the Jesuits to send him to China. They had gone there to tell the native people about their religion. The Jesuits, however, did not think he was ready, so La Salle quit his teaching job.

In search of an exciting new job, La Salle thought about going to New France. At the time, New France was a wild and dangerous place. The native people of the area, the Iroquois, were a powerful group of tribes.

Sieur de La Salle

The Iroquois had sworn revenge on the French for murdering two of their leaders several years before. The people who lived in unsettled areas west of the French settlement at Montreal lived in constant fear of war with the natives.

On the other hand, New France was also full of opportunity. Any Frenchman willing to settle there received land. And many—including one of La Salle's cousins—were getting rich trading furs.

As far as La Salle was concerned, New France offered a chance for excitement and wealth. And there were even rumors that somewhere in this unexplored land was a route to the Pacific Ocean. Maybe, La Salle thought, he would be able to find a way to China.

La Salle quickly established his own colony outside Montreal. As villages of French settlers and local natives were built, La Salle soon became a rich and powerful man. Still, it was not enough to satisfy him. La Salle had no interest in settling down, and no interest in living the life of a rich gentleman. He liked to be by himself, and he longed for more adventure.

In later life René-Robert Cavelier became known as Sieur de La Salle.

Then one day in 1668, some visiting natives told La Salle about a great river to the southwest. They called it the Ohio, or "Beautiful Water," and said it flowed into the sea. La Salle wondered if this was the western passage to China. Excitedly, he began making plans to find out.

The Search for Beautiful Water

On July 6, 1669, La Salle and 30 other men set off in birch bark canoes in search of the Ohio. If he could have, La Salle would have gone alone into the wilderness. He had no patience with others and no interest in what they thought or had to
say. But he needed strong men to carry supplies. He needed natives who knew the country to guide him.

The governor, or ruler, of New France had sent two priests, Father Galinee and Father Dollier, to travel with him. The priests had also heard of the Ohio, and wanted to tell the natives who lived there about the Christian religion.

La Salle went in search of the Ohio River.

La Salle explored for many months. The expedition slept in tents made of tree bark and ate boiled corn. But La Salle and his men still had not found the Ohio River.

The explorers stopped at one native village, hoping that the people there could help them. But instead the natives told them not to continue their journey. They said that the Ohio was far, far away, and that the people who lived along it would not like the strangers to be there.

La Salle did not believe them, but many of his men did. However, before they could quit and turn around, a hunter from a neighboring tribe passed through the village. He told La Salle that he knew the river and that his people could help them.

The native people were friendly toward La Salle and his men. However, they told La Salle to give up his search for the Ohio River.

La Salle followed the man to his village. There he was given a native from another tribe to lead him to the Ohio River. But La Salle made a surprising discovery. He and his men were not the only explorers in the area.

A Frenchman named Louis Jolliet was on his way back to Montreal after exploring the western Great Lakes. He told La Salle and the two priests about his journey. He also told them about a tribe of native people he had met. The priests decided to change their plans. They would find this tribe and tell them about the Christian religion. They told La Salle they would go west instead of south.

La Salle had little interest in finding these native people. His heart was set on finding the Ohio, and he was too close to give up now. He told the priests he would not go with them. He lied to them, saying that he was too sick. He said he would stay put until he was better, then go back to Montreal. However, as soon as the priests left, La Salle went off in search of the Ohio River.

It was two years before La Salle finally returned to Montreal. Because the records of that time in his life have all been lost, no one is certain what he did during those years.

Experts think that La Salle probably did find the Ohio River, and maybe even the Illinois River. The sight of these fertile valleys may even have convinced the explorer that his future lay in this part of North America.

LA SALLE'S JOURNEYS IN NORTH AMERICA

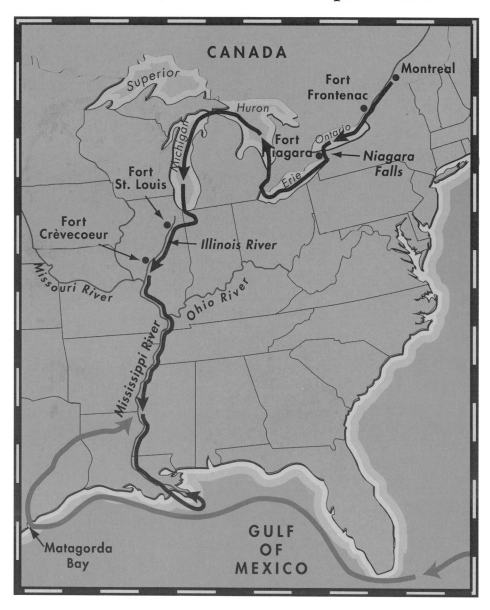

A New Dream

When La Salle finally returned to New France, he was surprised to find a new governor there. His name was Louis de Buade, comte de Frontenac. "Comte" is the French word for "count." Like La Salle, Frontenac believed there was much to be gained—for France and for his own pocket—in the unexplored center of the continent. Frontenac wanted to see France's empire extend farther south and west. And to La Salle's delight, he believed the young explorer was the man to bring this about.

As a first step, Frontenac asked La Salle to build a fort near Lake Ontario. La Salle did, and named it Fort Frontenac. Within a few years it became a successful colony. This made La Salle one of the most powerful men in Canada. But he was also one of the most disliked. Many landowners and traders in New France thought he was unfriendly. They were also jealous of his friendship with the new governor. But La Salle didn't care. He didn't like most people, and he didn't care if they liked him.

Once Fort Frontenac was set up, La Salle began looking for something else to do. Before long, he got word that Louis Jolliet and a Jesuit priest named Jacques Marquette had explored a river to the southwest. The native peoples called it the Missi-Sepe, or "Big Water." Today it is known as the Mississippi River. Afraid of running into Spanish soldiers, Jolliet and Marquette had turned around at the point where the Mississippi and the Arkansas rivers meet. But the two explorers had gone far enough to know that the Mississippi flowed south into the Gulf of Mexico.

When La Salle heard this, he became excited. For years he had dreamed of finding a waterway through the continent to the Pacific Ocean—a Northwest Passage. But a river from the north all the way to the south might be just as good. It would mean that ships loaded with treasures from the rich land could sail back to Europe through the Gulf of Mexico. Goods would not have to be carried through the rough ground of Canada. And if France controlled that river, it would control a rich empire almost as big as Europe.

La Salle knew that in order to control the Mississippi, France would have to build colonies along it. It was a huge task for one man to do. But La Salle was determined. He wanted to be the man to establish those colonies—and rule the empire they created.

With Frontenac's help, La Salle sailed to France. He asked King Louis XIV to allow him to lead an expedition all the way to the Mississippi's mouth. He told the king he would explore the land and make friends with the native peoples who lived there. He would build forts and establish colonies. And most importantly, he would claim all that land for France before Spain or England could get there.

Louis Jolliet and Jacques Marquette explored the Mississippi River.

Naturally, it sounded like a good plan to the king, especially since La Salle would raise all the money he needed by himself. Louis XIV told La Salle yes, and the explorer hurried back to New France to prepare for the expedition.

La Salle with King Louis XIV of France

The Greater the Danger, the Greater the Honor

La Salle did not return to New France alone. With him came more than 30 men. With more men to assist him and boatloads of supplies, La Salle headed for Niagara Falls. This is a waterfall on the Niagara River, about halfway between Lake Erie and Lake Ontario. There he ordered a huge ship to be built to carry his expedition west to Lake Michigan. La Salle named the ship the *Griffon*, after a make-

Niagara Falls

believe creature that is half eagle and half lion. This was the beast drawn on Count Frontenac's coat of arms.

On August 7, 1679, the *Griffon* became the first ship to sail across Lake Erie. La Salle's plan was to sail to Lake Michigan, collecting valuable furs along the way. Then he would have a fort built on the St. Joseph River, or Miamis River, as the local natives called it.

In the meantime, the captain of the *Griffon* would sail back to Fort Niagara and sell the furs. Then he would return with fresh supplies and materials for building a second ship. The men would take these materials to the Illinois River. Then they would spend the winter building the second ship. In the spring, La Salle would sail that ship down the Mississippi, into the Gulf of Mexico, and on to France!

Unfortunately, La Salle's plan ran into problems. Though he waited and waited, the *Griffon* never arrived. For the first time in his life, the self-confident explorer began to get nervous. The weather was growing colder and the rivers were starting to freeze. Soon La Salle and his men would be snowed in at the fort on the St. Joseph River that they called Fort Miamis. They would not have any food or real shelter. At last, La Salle decided he could not wait any longer. He did not know—and never found out—what had happened to the *Griffon*. But he had to move on.

The journey over land to the Illinois River was dangerous. The snow was deep, and there was little food. If La Salle's men had not found buffalo in a swamp, they might have starved.

Finding buffalo saved La Salle's men from starving.

La Salle drove his men on for four long weeks, until they reached the Illinois River valley and the hunting ground of the group of native people called the Illinois.

By then, most of La Salle's men had grown to dislike their stern leader. They felt he worked them too hard. When he spoke to them, it was to bark orders or scold them. But usually he ignored them altogether.

On the other hand, the Illinois welcomed La Salle warmly. They seemed to like his serious manner and expression. He had carried a calumet, or peace pipe, with him from Canada, and greeted the Illinois with it. He also gave them gifts.

La Salle explained that his chief, the King of France, had sent him to travel down the Mississippi and bring back goods to trade with them.

This made the Illinois a little suspicious. They didn't like the idea of Frenchmen taking over their trading territory. They fed the weary Frenchmen fresh buffalo meat and entertained them with dances. But they also tried to discourage them from going any farther. They told La Salle's men frightening stories of fierce tribes that lived along the Mississippi River and of monsters living in its waters.

A calumet, or peace pipe

La Salle told his men that these tales were not true. And besides, he said, "the greater the danger, the greater the honor." They would explore the Mississippi. And they would do it in a big ship, just as he had planned. So what if there was still no word from the *Griffon*? He would just go back 1,000 miles (1,600 km) to Canada to get more supplies.

Starting Over

On March 1, 1680, La Salle set off with a small group of men for Fort Frontenac. With him was an Italian officer named Henri de Tonti. Tonti had lost his right arm in battle years before and wore an iron claw in its place. He was fearless and loyal, and would become one of the few men La Salle could trust.

La Salle left Tonti in charge of the fort. La Salle had called it Fort Crèvecoeur (or "Heartbreak" in English). La Salle took two canoes, but they did him little good. The frozen rivers were just starting to thaw. La Salle and his men spent most of their trip sick, hungry, and knee-deep in icy mud.

This was not La Salle's only problem. When he finally reached Fort Frontenac, he learned that some people to whom he owed money had taken everything he'd left behind. They were sure he would never return to Canada alive. Then Tonti sent a letter saying that the men who had been left at Fort Crèvecoeur had rebelled. They had robbed the fort and planned to do the same to Fort Miamis.

La Salle borrowed more money, hired new men, and filled the canoes with new supplies. He then returned to the Illinois valley, ready to get back to work. But the valley he returned to was completely different from the one he had left. Not only was Fort Crèvecoeur destroyed, but the nearby Illinois village was also burned to the ground. And Tonti was nowhere to be found.

Before La Salle could go on, he had to find Tonti. When he did, his friend told him that the Iroquois had heard about La Salle's plans. They had also heard about his friendship with the Illinois. That made them angry and they destroyed the village. Tonti told La Salle that he had been lucky to escape with his life.

However, Tonti still wanted to go on La Salle's expedition. This time, La Salle decided they would not worry about building a ship. They would sail the Mississippi in canoes. And a few months later, in February 1682, La Salle, Tonti, and a new crew of Frenchmen and native guides set off.

As the men made their way down the mighty river, it was clear that the stories the Illinois had told them were not true. They had seen a few crocodiles here and there, but no terrible monsters. And the native tribes were friendly to them. A group of native people called the

Arkansas helped the explorers build shelters and brought them firewood. Another group called the Taensas welcomed them into a city as big as any in New France. Many other native tribes offered whatever help they could.

La Salle on the Mississippi River

In every native village, La Salle offered his calumet as a sign of friendship and handed out gifts. Then he claimed the land around the villages for France.

On April 9, La Salle made the grandest and boldest claim of all. On a patch of high, dry land near the Gulf of Mexico, La Salle's men fired muskets and shouted, "Long live the king!" The explorer planted a plaque in the ground. Then he claimed an area as big as 14 states today for his homeland.

From that day on, La Salle declared, all the "seas, harbors, ports, bays, adjacent straits, and all the nations, peoples, provinces, cities, towns, villages, mines, minerals, fisheries, streams, and rivers, from the Gulf of Mexico to its end" would belong to Louis XIV, king of France. In his honor, this land would be called Louisiana.

La Salle claimed the territory surrounding the Mississippi River for France.

Fort St. Louis

Of course, claiming the Louisiana Territory was just the first step for La Salle. He still had to establish colonies at both ends of the Mississippi.

La Salle started back up the river right away. But it was slow going against the Mississippi's mighty current. The expedition's food supply soon ran out. For weeks they had nothing to eat but alligator meat. La Salle himself became very ill. Forced to stop and rest for more than a month, he sent Tonti ahead. He was to begin work on a fort that would be called St. Louis.

In spite of his illness, the explorer was not discouraged. Nor was he discouraged when he caught up with Tonti. His friend told him that Frontenac had been replaced by a new governor. And this man would not support La Salle's ideas.

La Salle had come too far to see his plans fall through. If the governor in New France would not help him, he would go straight to the king. In 1683, La Salle set sail once again for France.

La Salle convinced King Louis XIV to give him the right to settle the land along the Mississippi.

It was not hard for La Salle to convince King Louis XIV again that having colonies on the Mississippi was exactly what France needed. First, it was the only way to control this important river. Second, it was a sure way to take lands in the west away from France's rival, Spain. The king quickly ordered the new governor to go along with La Salle's plan. He also gave the explorer four ships loaded with supplies and 300 soldiers, sailors, carpenters, and colonists who would help him build a fort at the mouth of the Mississippi.

On July 24, 1684, La Salle set sail once more. This time he did not go to Canada. He headed directly for the Gulf of Mexico and the mouth of the Mississippi. Unfortunately, finding the Mississippi this way was not easy. The voyage took much longer than La Salle had planned. But finally, after looking for the mouth of the river for six months and losing two ships, La Salle landed.

By then, the colonists had nothing left to eat but flour. The place where they landed had little fresh water and no wood. Every day, five or six colonists died. But La Salle did not have time to mourn the dead or comfort the living. He put everyone to work building another Fort St. Louis. As far as La Salle was concerned, if he could carry on, they could too.

Only later did La Salle realize that he had not found the right river. In fact, he had gone 400 miles (640 km) too far. His ships had traveled all the way to Matagorda Bay in present-day Texas. And his party's hardships were just beginning. They still had to find the Mississippi.

La Salle landed in Matagorda Bay by mistake.

An End . . .
and a
Beginning

La Salle decided to take his third ship and try to find the Mississippi by sailing along the coast. The fourth boat, a large ship with cannons, had already sailed for France to rejoin the French navy. Before La Salle could find the Mississippi, however, he became very ill. And if that were not bad enough, while he was still recovering, his last boat was wrecked in choppy seas.

La Salle returned to Fort St. Louis on foot. When he arrived, he found his colonists in even worse shape than before. La Salle could not cheer them. He did not know how. But he was determined to try and save them. He would try to find the Mississippi once again. Then he would follow it north to Canada and get help.

On a bright spring day in 1686, La Salle's colonists watched him set off with 20 of his strongest men. But a few months later, he returned with a ragged crew of only eight men. He was almost too weak and sick to give them the bad news that they had not found the Mississippi.

La Salle tried in vain to find the mouth of the Mississippi.

The colonists still had hope that the fourth ship would send help back from France. But two years had passed since the ship left. If a rescue ship had not come yet, it probably never would. To save what was left of Fort St. Louis, La Salle would have to try again to get to Canada.

In January 1687, La Salle set off with another search party. After two months of looking for, and not finding, the Mississippi River, La Salle's weary crew decided they'd had enough of La Salle's miserable journey, and of him.

On March 15, a group of men left La Salle's camp to hunt for food. They were a few miles north of where Houston, Texas, is today. Four days later, hungry and impatient, La Salle went out looking for them. The men were waiting. As their leader approached, they jumped out of the tall grass and shot him in the head.

It was more than a year before La Salle's body was discovered. By then, Fort St. Louis of Texas had just about disappeared. Experts do not know if the colonists died of disease and hunger, or if they found some local natives to help them. But when Spanish soldiers found the fort in 1689, it had been deserted for some time.

La Salle was killed by his own men.

In spite of La Salle's sad ending, his work was not useless. Because of his dreams and hard work, the city of New Orleans was built by the French 30 years later. And until it was sold to the United States in 1803, the Louisiana Territory made France the richest nation that had claimed land in the Americas.

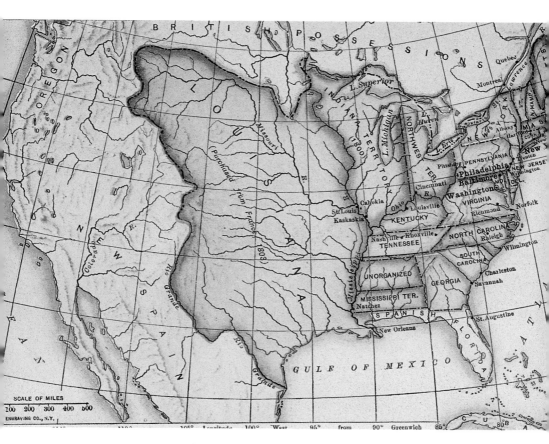

A map showing the United States in 1803

Other Events of the 17th Century
(1601 – 1700)

During the century that Sieur de La Salle was exploring North America, events were happening in other parts of the world. Some of these were:

1608   French explorer Samuel Champlain founds the settlement of New France in what is now Canada.

1632   Italian scientist Galileo Galilei supports the idea that the sun, and not the Earth, is the center of the solar system.

1642–1649   King Charles I of England and the country's parliament fight for leadership. The conflict is known as the English Civil War.

1643   The Taj Mahal, a building surrounded by gardens, is completed in India. Emperor Shah Jahan had it built in memory of his wife.

1644   Ch'ing Dynasty is established in China.

1652   Foundation of Cape Colony by the Dutch.

1659   French found trading station on Senegal coast of Africa.

Time Line

November 21, 1643	René-Robert Cavelier (Sieur de La Salle) is born in Rouen, France.
Spring 1666	La Salle sails to New France (Canada).
July 1669	La Salle sets off in search of the Ohio River.
1670-1672	La Salle continues searching for the Ohio River.
Summer 1672	Louis Jolliet and Father Jacques Marquette come to the Mississippi River.
1673	La Salle builds Fort Frontenac near present-day Kingston, Ontario.
Fall 1677	La Salle sails to France and asks King Louis XIV to let him explore the Mississippi.
August 1679	La Salle's expedition sets sail on the *Griffon*.
March 1680	La Salle returns to Fort Frontenac on foot.

Winter 1681	La Salle sets off on his second expedition to explore the Mississippi.
February 1682	La Salle reaches the Mississippi.
April 9, 1682	La Salle reaches the Gulf of Mexico. He claims the area, called the Louisiana Territory, for France.
Spring 1684	La Salle returns to France. He asks King Louis XIV to let him build a colony at the mouth of the Mississippi.
July 1684	La Salle sets sail with four ships and 400 people. They head for the Gulf of Mexico.
February 1685	La Salle lands at Matagorda Bay, Texas. This is 400 miles (640 km) beyond the mouth of the Mississippi.
April 1686	La Salle sets off on foot to find the Mississippi.
January 1687	La Salle sets off on foot a second time to find the Mississippi.
March 19, 1687	La Salle is killed by members of his party.

GLOSSARY

bay A part of the ocean partly enclosed by land

calumet (KAL-yuh-met) Another name for a peace pipe

colony (KOL-uh-nee) An area that has been settled by people from another country and is governed by that country

comte (KAHMT) The French word for "count"

continent (KON-tuh-nent) One of the seven great landmasses (North America, South America, Africa, Asia, Europe, Australia, Antarctica)

empire (EM-pire) A large territory that is under the rule of one leader

expedition (ek-spuh-DISH-un) A trip for a special purpose, such as to explore or take over lands

Fort Crèvecoeur (KREV-kur) A fort built by La Salle on the Illinois River

Fort Frontenac (FRON-tuh-nak) A fort built by La Salle on Lake Ontario

Fort Miamis (mi-A-meez) A fort built by La Salle on the St. Joseph River

Great Lakes A group of five lakes (Superior, Michigan, Huron, Erie, and Ontario) in the center of North America

gulf A part of the ocean that reaches into the land

Iroquois (EER-uh-kwoi) A powerful native tribe who were enemies of the French in North America

Jesuits (JEH-zoo-uts) The most educated and adventurous group of missionaries of the Catholic Church

Louisiana Territory (loo-ee-zee-AH-nuh TER-uh-tor-ee) The area of North America claimed for France by La Salle, basically the Mississippi River Valley

missionaries (MISH-uh-nehr-eez) People sent by a church or religious group to teach that group's faith and do good works

New France The part of North America that was claimed by the French. Today it is called Canada.

Niagara Falls (ni-AH-gruh) A waterfall on the Niagara River, about halfway between Lake Erie and Lake Ontario

Northwest Passage (PASS-ij) A sea route connecting the Atlantic and Pacific Oceans along the northern coast of North America

sieur (SYUR) A French title that means "sir" in English

strait (STRAYT) A narrow waterway that connects two larger bodies of water

Taensas (TAH-en-sus) A group of native people that lived along the Mississippi River during La Salle's time

Index